Black Beauty

Anna Sewell

Condensed and Adapted by
LOUISE COLLN

Illustrated by
MICHEAL FISHER

Cover Illustrated by
EZRA TUCKER

bendon

The Junior Classics have been
adapted and illustrated with care and thought
to introduce you to a world of famous authors, characters, ideas,
and great stories that have been loved for generations.

Editor — Kathryn Knight
Creative Director — Gina Rhodes Haynes
And the entire classics project team
of Bendon Publishing

FOREWORD

A note to the reader—

A classic story rests in your hands. The characters are famous. The tale is timeless.

This Junior Classic edition of *Black Beauty* has been carefully condensed and adapted from the original version (which you really *must* read when you're ready for every detail). We kept the well-known phrases for you. We kept Anna Sewell's style. And we kept the important imagery and heart of the tale.

Literature is terrific fun! It encourages you to think. It helps you dream. It is full of heroes and villains, suspense and humor, adventure and wonder, and new ideas. It introduces you to writers who reach out across time to say: "Do you want to hear a story I wrote?"

Curl up and enjoy.

CONTENTS

CHARACTERS

I am BLACK BEAUTY — a horse with a story to tell

The Meadow—my first home
   FARMER GREY — my first owner
   MY MOTHER — a proud and noble mare who taught me well
   DANIEL — my first groom who worked for Farmer Grey

At Birtwick Park
   SQUIRE GORDON — my next owner, a fair and good man
   MISTRESS GORDON — the Squire's kind wife
   MISS FLORA AND MISS JESSIE — the two little Gordon girls
   GINGER — my good friend, a tall chestnut mare with a sad past
   MERRYLEGS — a gray pony for the children
   JOHN MANLY — the Squire's groom, an upright man
   JAMES HOWARD — the Squire's stable boy
   MR. BLOOMFIELD — the town minister
   LITTLE JOE GREEN — the stable boy after James left

At Earlshall Park
   THE EARL OF WILBURN — my new owner

LADY WILBURN — the Earl's fashionable but thoughtless wife

MISTER YORK — the Earl's head groom

LADY ANNE — a relative of the Wilburns who called me Black Auster

COLLIN BLANTYRE — Lady Anne's cousin

LIZZIE — a riding mare at Earlshall

REUBEN SMITH — a fine groom with one sad fault

ROBERT AND NED — the stable boys

My Days as a Work Horse

JERRY — a kind and good owner, a London cab driver, who called me Jack

POLLY — Jerry's merry wife

HARRY AND DOLLY — Jerry's children

CAPTAIN — a cab horse of Jerry's

MISTRESS FOWLER — a wealthy woman who knows Jerry and Polly

THE BAKER — a new owner

JAKES — the Baker's driver who called me Blackie

NICHOLAS SKINNER — a cruel owner with a set of cabs for hire

FARMER THOROUGHGOOD — a kind gent

WILLIE — the farmer's grandson who called me Old Crony

Black Beauty

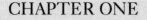

CHAPTER ONE

My Early Home

The first place that I can well remember was a large pleasant meadow. There was a pond of clear water in the meadow. Some shady trees grew beside the pond and water lilies grew at the deep end. At the top of the meadow was an orchard. At the bottom, a little brook sang along.

On one side of the meadow we looked over a hedge of green shrubs onto a field. On another side we saw Farmer Grey's house. I believe that it was the most pleasant place in all England to play and learn.

In the daytime I ran by my mother's side and at night I lay down close by her. When it was hot,

we used to stand in the shade beside the pond. When it was cold, we had a nice warm shed near the grove.

As soon as I was old enough to eat grass, my mother used to go out to pull Farmer Grey's carts. I played with the other colts in the meadow. We had great fun, but sometimes our play was a little rough.

One day my mother called me to her.

"Listen to me," she said. "You come from a good family of horses. You must learn good manners. You have never seen me kick or bite. I hope you will grow up gentle and good and never learn bad ways. Do your work with a good will, lift your feet up well when you trot, and never bite or kick, even in play." My mother was a wise old horse. I have never forgotten her advice.

There was a day I have never forgotten, too. I stood very close to my mother that day. A group of dogs ran by making high howling noises. We saw a poor frightened rabbit running from them.

Hunters on horses went galloping behind them. A horse and his rider tried to jump a stream in the field beyond ours. The horse fell and threw his rider. Both of them were hurt so badly that they died. All for one little rabbit.

My mother was much troubled. "It's only for sport that they were killed," she said. "Why do men take chances for themselves and for their horses? They chase a fox or rabbit that they don't need for food. But we are only horses and don't understand."

I thought my mother understood the matter better than the hunters did.

When I was older, Farmer Grey sent me to a neighbor's farm. I was put into a meadow with some sheep and cows. Train tracks ran on the other side of the fence. Farmer Grey wanted me to learn to not be afraid of the train.

I shall never forget the first train that ran past us. There was a rush and a clatter and a puffing of smoke. It looked like a long, black monster racing by. I galloped to the far side of the meadow as fast as I could. I stood snorting and pawing with fear. The cows and sheep hardly raised their heads. I thought that they might know something about the train.

I learned that they did. This terrible creature could do me no harm. It never came into the field, and so I began to pay no attention to it.

Very soon I paid no more attention to the train than the cows and sheep did. The noise when it stopped at a nearby station was loud. I soon stopped paying attention to that also.

When I returned home, my mother told me that I had learned two lessons. "You will be near trains when you start pulling carriages. Now you know not to be afraid. You won't be uneasy around them. The other lesson is good also. Get to know about the thing you are afraid of. It will often turn out to not be as scary as you thought."

When I became four years old, I was considered very handsome. My coat had grown fine and soft, and was bright black. I had one white foot, and a pretty white star on my forehead. A patch of white hair sparkled right in the middle of my back. Also I had learned good manners from my mother. Farmer Grey and Daniel considered me to be a good horse. Daniel was the groom who cared for the horses. I was happy to please him, for he was good to me.

One day Squire Gordon from Birtwick Park came to look at me. He looked at my eyes, my mouth, my back, and my legs. Then I walked, trotted, and galloped for him.

"When he has been broken in, I will buy him," he told Farmer Grey.

"I will break him in myself," Farmer Grey said. "I do not want him to be frightened or hurt."

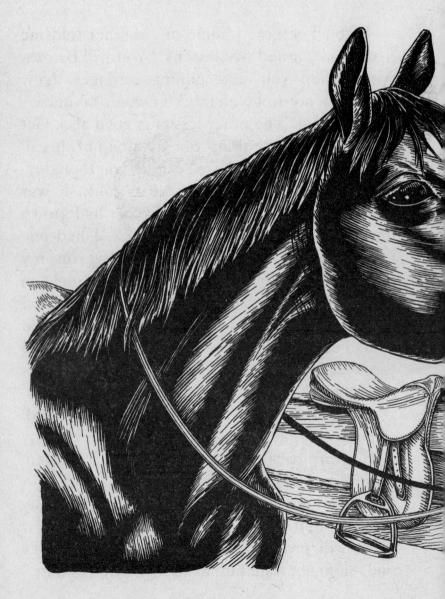

Farmer Grey first taught me to wear a saddle and a bridle. I did not like the steel bar he put in my mouth. He called it a "bit." It was a lump of cold, hard steel over my tongue. Farmer Grey was patient and gentle with me. I learned to let him put the bit in my mouth. One day he got in the saddle and rode on my back. It felt strange, but I soon learned to enjoy carrying him.

It was hard to stand still while a harness was put on me. All the pieces of steel and leather felt very heavy and tight. Afterwards, a cart or a carriage was fastened behind me. I had to get used to having it at my heels.

One day the blacksmith nailed iron shoes to my hooves. It didn't hurt and my mother told me they protected my feet. My feet felt very heavy at first, but I soon got used to them. I was glad to have my feet protected.

I knew that all grown-up horses wore this harness. I learned to not dislike it too much. Later I started pulling farm carts and carriages. Farmer Grey had my mother pull them beside me. She was steady and taught me very well.

"The better you behave, the better you will be treated," she told me. "Lift your feet when

you trot and try to please your owner. I hope you will have good owners. A horse cannot choose who may drive him. It is all chance for us. Still I say behave well, wherever you are."

With patience from Farmer Grey, I got used to everything. Soon I could work as well as my mother.

CHAPTER TWO

Birtwick Park

In early May I was sold to my owner's friend, Squire Gordon.

"Good-bye. Be a good horse and always do your best," Farmer Grey told me. He gave me a last kind pat on my neck.

Squire Gordon's large home was called Birtwick Park. We entered by a large iron gate. Then we trotted down a smooth road between clumps of big old trees. This brought us to the house and the gardens. Beyond this lay a small field with a fence around it. Inside the field was an old orchard with apple trees. The stables were near them.

The stables had room for many horses and carriages. My stall was large and clean. I had a new groom to care for me. He gave me some oats, patted me, and spoke kindly. Then he went away.

A tall chestnut mare stared angrily from a stall across from me. "I *was* in that stall," she said. "*You* took it from me."

"I beg your pardon," I said. "I had nothing to do with it. The groom put me here."

"Ginger has a bad habit of biting," said another voice, "and when she was in the loose stall, she used to snap very much. Miss Flora and Miss Jessie, who are very fond of me, were afraid to come into the stable. They used to bring me apples and carrots and I miss them very much."

I looked into the stall next to me. A little fat gray pony with a thick mane and tail stood there.

"My name is Merrylegs," he said. "I carry the young girls on my back. I miss the good things to eat and I hope the young ladies will come again—if *you* don't bite."

"I never bite anything but oats and corn and grass," I said.

"I bite because no one has been kind to me," Ginger, the chestnut mare, said.

"You may have been hurt *before* you came here," Merrylegs replied. "But our John Manly is the best groom that ever was. James Howard is a kind stable boy. You may learn to be good-tempered here. There is no better place for a horse to be."

The next morning Squire Gordon came to the stables. "Take the new horse out this morning to try him out."

"I will, sir," said John Manly.

He fitted me with a bridle and was very careful to make it comfortable. Then he found a saddle that fitted nicely. He rode slowly at first. Then we went faster at a trot, then a gallop.

As we came back through Birtwick Park, we met Squire and Mistress Gordon walking. They stopped and John jumped off.

"Well, John, how does he go?"

"First rate, sir," John answered. "He is as fast as a deer, and has a fine spirit. The lightest touch of the rein will guide him."

"That is very well," said Squire Gordon. "Tomorrow I will ride him."

The next day, I tried to do what Squire Gordon wanted. I found that he was a very good

rider. When we came home, Mistress Gordon waited at the door.

"He really is a good horse," Squire Gordon said. "What shall we call him?"

"He is beautiful. Shall we call him Black Beauty?"

And so Black Beauty became my name.

John seemed very proud of me. He brushed me and talked to me a great deal. "You really are a Beauty," he would say.

He seemed to know just how a horse feels, and when he cleaned me, he knew the tender places, and the ticklish places. When he brushed my head, he went as carefully over my eyes as if they were his own. James, the stable boy, was just as gentle. I was in a good home.

Ginger and I worked together to pull the big carriage. She behaved very well and I liked her. She did her full share of work. Squire Gordon was pleased by the way we worked together.

CHAPTER THREE

Merrylegs and Ginger

Merrylegs and I soon became great friends. He was such a cheerful, plucky little fellow. Everyone loved him. Miss Jessie and Miss Flora rode him about the orchard and field. They had fine games with him and their little dog, Frisky.

Mr. Bloomfield, the minister, had a large family of boys and girls who often played with Miss Jessie and Flora. They liked to take turns getting on Merrylegs to ride.

One afternoon Merrylegs had been out with them for a long time. When James brought him in he said, "There, you bad boy. Mind how you behave yourself. You shall get us into trouble."

"What have you been doing, Merrylegs?" I asked.

"Oh, nothing much," said he, tossing his head. "I have only been giving those young people a lesson. They didn't know when to stop and let me rest. I just pitched them off backwards."

"What?" said I. "You threw the children off? I thought you knew better than that! Did you throw Miss Jessie or Miss Flora?"

He looked very hurt. "Of course not! I would never do such a thing. Not for the best oats that ever came into the stable. It is I who teach the little ones to ride. At first, I go as smooth as an old kitty when she is after a bird. When they have learned, I go on again faster. So don't you talk to me about that. I am the best friend these children will ever have."

"Then what *did* you do?" I asked.

"It was the boys," he said, shaking his mane. "The boys must be broken in and taught what is right. They are just as we were when we were colts. The other children had ridden me about for nearly two hours. Then the boys thought it was their turn. I was quite willing. I galloped them about for a good hour. They had each cut a big

stick for a riding whip. They laid it on a little too hard. At last it had gone on long enough, so I stopped two or three times by way of a hint.

"Boys, you see, think a pony is like a steam engine. They wanted me to go on as long as they pleased. They never think that a pony can get tired. The one who was whipping me could not understand. I just rose up on my hind legs and let him slip off behind. He mounted me again, and I did the same. Then the other boy got up on me. As soon as he began to use his whip, I laid him on the grass. I slipped them off until they could understand. That was all. Then they told James what I had done. I think he was very angry to see such big sticks."

"I would have given those boys a good kick," Ginger said. "That would have given them a lesson."

"Oh, no," said Merrylegs. "You know I would never do anything to make James unhappy. I love our family. I do."

He gave a low "ho, ho, ho" through his nose, just as he always did in the morning when he heard James at the stable door.

I often thought of Merrylegs' wise words and I believe Ginger did, too.

We were as good for riding as we were for driving, and liked to be saddled for a riding party. Riding all together always put us in high spirits.

I had the best of it, for I always carried Mistress Gordon. She weighed little and her voice was sweet. Her hand was so light on the reins that I was guided almost without feeling it.

I was proud to live at Birtwick Park. Squire and Mistress Gordon were good and kind. They were liked by everyone who knew them. Every creature had a friend in them.

I was quite happy, but there was one thing I missed. It was the freedom to run or lie down when I wished. A spirited young horse wants to fling up his head and gallop. It was hard never to have freedom to do as I liked.

John understood. "We'll get the ticklish fidgets out of your feet," he would say. Then he'd saddle me and ride me a few miles at a fast trot. After that I was willing to go back into the stables for a while.

Sometimes, on Sundays, we were turned out into the field. We would run or lie down, or nibble the sweet grass. We stood together under the shade of the apple trees. Sometimes we talked to each other.

One day Ginger told me her story. "No one was kind to me. I was taken from my mother when I was very young. The man who cared for us only gave us food and shelter. He never stroked us or spoke kindly."

The way she had been broken in to wear a saddle and be harnessed to a carriage had been harsh. Then she was sold to other owners who gave no thought to her comfort. She became very unhappy and began to bite and kick. "I was sold again and again until I came here," she said.

"Well," I said, "I think it would be a real shame if you were to bite or kick John or James."

"I did bite James once. I thought he would flog me. John said, 'Try her with kindness.' James brought me a bran mash and stroked me. I haven't snapped at him since. I won't ever again."

As the weeks went on, Ginger grew more gentle and cheerful. She stopped biting and never kicked.

The Squire noticed the change in her, too. He came up to her and stroked her beautiful neck.

"Well, my pretty one, how do things go with you now? You are much happier than when you first came to us."

"Yes, sir," John said. "She's much improved. She's not the same creature that she was. It's the Birtwick medicine, sir."

This was a little joke of John's. He said that the Birtwick medicine was made up of patience and gentleness. He added firmness and petting. It was to be given to each horse every day.

It was just a joke, but we horses enjoyed getting his medicine.

CHAPTER FOUR

A Stormy Day

One day late in the autumn, Squire Gordon needed to go to town on business. John and the Squire rode in a light, high-wheeled cart. I always enjoyed pulling it. It rolled along so easily.

There had been a lot of rain and the wind was blowing leaves across the road. We went along merrily until we came to the tollgate at a low wooden bridge, which went straight across a small river.

The man taking the toll money said the river was rising fast and that it might soon lap over the low bridge. He feared that it would be a bad night. Many of the meadows were under water.

In one low part of the road the water was almost up to my knees. I was not afraid. The Squire drove me through it carefully.

In town the Squire's business kept us waiting for a long time. It was late in the afternoon when we started home. We went along beside some woods. The big branches were swaying about like twigs. The rushing sound of the wind was terrible.

"I wish that we were out of these woods," said the Squire.

"Yes, sir, I do too," said John. "It would be terrible if one of these limbs came down on us."

Soon there was a groan, and a crack, and a splitting sound. A huge oak crashed on the road before us. The wind had torn it up by the roots. I stopped, trembling with fright. I knew better than to run. I was taught to stay when I should. John came to my head in a moment and I felt better as he rubbed my face.

"That was close," said the Squire. "What should we do now?"

John went to look at the tree. "The tree is very big. We can never get over it. We will be stuck in mud if we try to drive around it."

"We will have to go back to the crossroads," the Squire said. "It will be miles before we get back to the bridge."

"It will make us late, but Beauty is fresh," John said.

We went back and took another road to the bridge. By the time we got to the bridge it was very nearly dark. We could see that the water was over the middle. That was usual when the river was full. We would go slowly through the water. It would just be over my feet. Squire Gordon kept me going along.

My feet touched the first part of the bridge. I knew there was something wrong, and I dared not go forward. I stopped.

"Go on, Beauty," said Squire Gordon. He gave me a touch with the whip. I dared not stir. He gave me a sharp cut. I jumped but I dared not go forward.

"There is something wrong, sir," said John. He came to my head, and tried to lead me forward.

"Come on, Beauty, what is the matter?" he asked.

I did not know what was wrong. I just knew that the bridge was not safe. It did not feel right to my feet.

Just then the man at the tollgate on the other side ran out. He waved a lantern.

"Hoy, hoy, hoy, halloo, stop!" he cried.

"What is wrong?" shouted the Squire.

"The bridge is broken in the middle. Part of it is carried away. If you come on you will all go into the river."

"Beauty knew!" said the Squire. "Beauty knew something was wrong."

"You Beauty!" said John. He gently turned me around to get to another road. I trotted along easily.

I heard them talking behind me. They said that if I had gone onto the bridge we might have been drowned.

"People use their minds to find out things," the Squire said. "Animals have a wisdom that we don't understand. They save our lives sometimes."

When at last we came home, Mistress Gordon ran out. "Are you really safe, my dear? I have been so worried. Have you had an accident?"

"No, my dear," Squire Gordon said. "We would have if it weren't for Beauty's wisdom.

Your Black Beauty was wiser than we were. He kept us from falling in the river at the wooden bridge." He told her about our trip.

What a good supper John gave me that night. I had a good wet bran mash and some crushed beans with my oats. Then he gave me such a thick bed of straw. I was glad of it, for I was tired.

Some time after that, John and I were driving down a road. We saw a boy trying to leap a pony over a gate. The gate was so high that the pony couldn't jump it. The boy got off and gave the pony a hard thrashing. Then he got on again and tried to make him jump the gate. He even kicked the pony shamelessly.

The pony put down his head and threw up his heels. He sent the boy neatly over into a thorny hedge. Then he set off for home at a full gallop.

John laughed out quite loudly. "Served him right," he said.

"Oh! Oh! Oh!" cried the boy. His feet looked funny sticking up from the hedge. "Come and help me out."

"No, thank you," said John, "I think you are in the right place. A few scratches will teach you not to jump a pony over such a high gate."

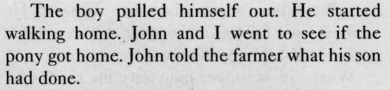

The boy pulled himself out. He started walking home. John and I went to see if the pony got home. John told the farmer what his son had done.

"He got a lesson from this," the father said. "He has mistreated that pony before. I shall stop him from mistreating the animal again."

We went on, John chuckling all the way home. When he told James about it, James said, "Served him right. My teacher at school talked to us often about cruelty. He said that it is mean and bad to hurt the weak and helpless. Good people are kind to man and beast. They are never cruel."

"Your teacher never taught you a truer thing," said John.

CHAPTER FIVE

The Fire

One December morning, John had just put me in my stall, when the Squire came into the stable. He looked serious. He said, "Good morning, John. I want to know if you have any complaint about James. Does he work hard and is he respectful?"

"Oh, yes, sir, always," John answered.

"He is never lazy when you turn your back?"

"Never, sir, and if anybody has been saying that about James, I don't believe it. No one can take away James's character. He is a steady, pleasant, honest, smart young fellow."

The Squire stood listening. Then a broad

smile spread over his face and he looked over to the doorway—where James had been standing the whole time.

"James, my lad," said the Squire, "I knew John would speak highly of you. Sir Williams is in need of a good young groom. You're to start in six weeks if you are pleased with the offer."

Though he would miss us all, James decided to train for the position. John and the Squire had him drive us often so he could learn more. At first, John rode with him on the driver's box, telling him this and that, and soon James drove alone. Then it was wonderful to go into the city on Saturday. The Squire would have James drive us through strange, interesting streets to get used to the busy traffic. He drove to the noisy railway station, even with cabs and carriages, carts and wagons all around us. James learned to be a very good driver.

Later, Squire and Mistress Gordon decided to visit some friends, and James drove Ginger and me. The first day we traveled thirty-two miles. There were some high hills, but James drove thoughtfully. He gave us a time to rest if the road was very steep.

At sunset we reached the town where we were to spend the night. We stopped at the best hotel. James took us to the hotel stables. Two grooms were in charge of caring for the horses.

The head groom was a pleasant, active little man with a crooked leg. With a pat and a good word, he led me to a long stall. The other man brought Ginger. James stood by while we were rubbed down and cleaned. I was never cleaned so fast and so well as I was by that little old man. James rubbed his hand over my back, and he found my coat as clean and smooth as silk.

"Well," James said, "I thought *I* was pretty fast. You are the *best* I have seen at grooming. You are fast and careful at the same time."

"Practice makes perfect," said the man. "I have had forty years practice. As to being fast, why, bless you! That is only a matter of habit. If you get into the habit of being fast, it goes easier than being slow. I've been with horses since I was twelve years old. I love them. I love seeing a well cared-for horse like this one."

He and James saw that the other groom had cared for Ginger. They brought out corn, and then they left the stable together.

Later on, the other groom brought in a traveler's horse. Another young man came into the stable to talk to him. The young man had a pipe in his mouth.

"I need more hay for the horses," the groom said. "Will you run up the ladder into the loft and throw some down? Only, lay down your pipe before you go up to the hayloft."

I heard the other man open a trap door. He stepped across the floor overhead, and then put down the hay.

James came in to check on us one last time. Then the stable door was locked and we horses went to sleep.

I woke up feeling very uncomfortable. The air seemed all thick and choking. I heard Ginger coughing. One of the other horses moved around in his stall. I could see nothing in the dark, for the stable was very full of smoke and I could hardly breathe.

The trap door to the loft above us had been left open. I heard a low crackling and snapping noise coming from overhead. There was something in the sound so strange that it made me tremble all over. The other horses were now all awake, pulling at their halters and stamping their feet.

At last I heard steps outside. The groom who had put up the traveler's horse ran into the stable. He began to untie the horses and try to lead them out, but he seemed so frightened himself that he frightened the horses still more. None of the horses would go with him. He tried to drag me out of my stall by force, but I was afraid and wouldn't stir. He tried us all by turns and then left the stable.

No doubt we were very foolish, but we were frightened. Danger seemed to be all around and there was nobody we could trust. Everything was strange and uncertain. The fresh air that had come in through the open door made it easier to breathe, but the sounds overhead grew louder. As I looked upward through the bars, I saw a red light flickering on the wall.

Then I heard a cry of "Fire" outside, and the old groomsman quietly and quickly came in. He got one horse out, and went to another, but the flames were leaping from the trap door and the roaring overhead was dreadful.

Then next thing I heard was James's voice,

sounding quiet and cheery as it always was. "Come, my beauties. It is time for us to be off. Wake up and come along."

He came to me first. "Come, Beauty, on with your bridle, my boy. We'll soon be out of this fire," he said, patting me.

The bridle was on in no time. Then he took the scarf off his neck and tied it lightly over my eyes. Patting and coaxing, he led me out of the stable.

Safe in the yard, he slipped the scarf off my eyes. "Here, somebody!" he shouted. "Take this horse while I go back for the other."

A tall man took my bridle as James darted back into the stable. I sent up a shrill whinny as I saw him go.

There was confusion in the yard. Horses were being led out. Carriages were being pulled out of the sheds. People were shouting all about me, but I kept my eyes fixed on the stable door. The smoke poured out thicker than ever, and I could see flashes of red light.

In a little while I heard Squire Gordon's voice above all the noise. "James! James Howard! Are you there?"

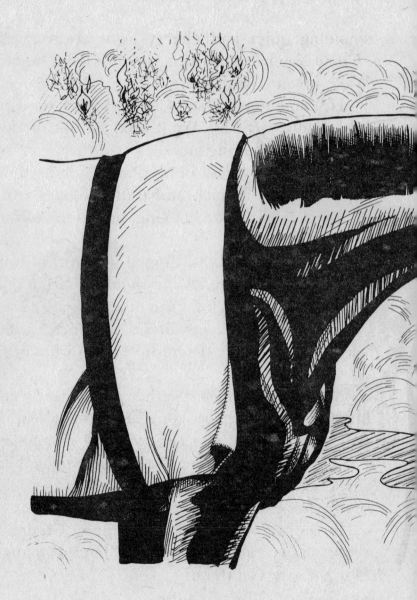

There was no answer. I heard a crash of something falling inside the stable. Then I gave a loud, joyful neigh, for I saw James coming through the smoke leading Ginger. She was coughing and he was unable to speak.

"My brave lad!" said the Squire. He put his hand on James's shoulder. "Are you hurt?"

James shook his head, for he still could not speak.

"Yes, indeed," said the man who held me, "he is a brave lad. Your horses know whom they can trust."

"Rest a moment and catch your breath," said the Squire. "Then we'll get out of this place as quickly as we can."

Suddenly, from the Market Place, there came a sound of galloping feet and loud rumbling wheels.

"It's the fire engine! The fire engine!" shouted several voices. "Stand back! Make way!"

Two horses clattered over the stone street and dashed into the yard pulling the fire engine behind them. The firemen leaped to the ground. They started pumping to force water onto the burning roof.

It was too late. The roof crashed down on everything inside.

We went to another hotel where we were put into safe stalls. James went back to find out more about the fire. He found out that the careless man who had gone up into the loft to throw down the hay had started it with his pipe. Two poor horses were buried under the burnt roof.

Ginger told me that my whinny saved her that night. When she heard me, she knew I was safely outside. That gave her the courage to follow James.

CHAPTER SIX

Going for the Doctor

Our journey was put off until afternoon. We stayed a few days with the friends, then had an easy journey back home. We were very glad to get back to our own stables. John was glad to see us, especially after James told him about the fire. Then James asked him who was coming to take his place.

"Little Joe Green at the lodge," said John.

"Little Joe Green? Why, he is a child!"

"He is fourteen and a half," said John.

"But he is such a little chap!"

"Yes, he is small, but he is quick and willing to learn. He is kind-hearted, too, and wishes very much to come, and his father would like it. I know the Squire would like to give him the chance. I have agreed to try him for six weeks."

"Six weeks!" said James. "Why, it will be six months before he can be of much use! Training him will be a lot of work for you, John."

"Well," said John with a laugh, "work and I are very good friends. I never was afraid of work yet."

"You are a very good man," said James. "I wish I may ever be like you."

"I don't often speak of myself," said John, "but since you are leaving, I'll tell you how I look on these things. I was just as old as Joe when my father and mother died and left me and my sister Nelly alone in the world. We would have gone to the workhouse if the Gordons had not hired us. Nelly did knitting and needlework. The Squire took me in as a stable boy. His coachman, old Norman, trained me. Norman *could* have said that at *his* age he wouldn't train a young boy, but he was like a father to me. He took time to train me. When Norman died some years after, I stepped into his place. And now I earn enough for me and Nelly—and am even able to save for my later years.

"So you see, James, I am not a man who would turn up his nose at a little boy. No, no! I shall miss you very much, James, but we shall pull through. There's nothing like doing a kindness for someone else, and I am glad I can do it."

"Then," said James, "you don't go by that saying, 'Everybody look after himself, and take care of number one'?"

"No, indeed," said John. "Where would Nelly and I have been if Squire and Mrs. Gordon and old Norman had only taken care of number one? Why, in the workhouse. And where would Black Beauty and Ginger have been if you had only thought of number one? Why, left in the burning stable! No, Jim, no! That is a selfish saying. And any man who thinks he has nothing to do but take care of number one, why, he will only lead a sad life—that's what I think," said John, with a very firm nod of his head.

James smiled at this. But there was a sadness in his voice when he said, "You have been my best friend except my mother. I hope you won't forget me."

"No, lad, no!" said John. "And if ever I can do you a good turn I hope you won't forget me."

The next day, young Joe came to the stable to learn all he could before James left. He swept the stable and brought in the straw and hay. He learned to clean the harnesses, and helped to wash the carriage. He was too short to groom Ginger and me, so James taught him to groom Merrylegs. He was a nice little bright fellow, and always came whistling to his work.

James was sad on the day he had to leave us. We liked Joe, but were also sorry to see James go.

One night, a few days after James had left, I was asleep on my straw when the stable bell rang. I heard the door of John's house open, and his feet running up to the hall. He was back again in no time. He unlocked the stable door and came in, calling out, "Wake up, Beauty!"

He saddled and bridled me and took me to Squire Gordon.

The Squire said with great concern, "Now, John, you must ride for your life—that is, for Mrs. Gordon's life, for there is not a moment to lose. Ride to Doctor White and give him this note. Ride as fast as you can. Let Beauty rest at the doctor's stable, and then be back as soon as you can."

Off we raced down the road, through the village, and up the hill until we came to the toll-gate. John called very loudly and thumped on the door. The man came out and flung open the gate.

"Now," said John, "keep the gate open for when the doctor comes back this way. Here is the money for his toll."

There was a long level road by the riverside. John said to me, "Now, Beauty, do your best." And so I did. I galloped as fast as I could lay my feet to the ground.

The air was frosty, the moon was bright, and it was very pleasant. We came through a dark wood, then uphill and downhill. After an eight-mile run we came to the town. We stopped at Doctor White's door just as the clock struck three. John rang the bell twice. Then he knocked at the door like thunder. Doctor White, in his nightcap, put his head out his window.

"What do you want?" he called.

"Mrs. Gordon is very ill, sir. The Squire wants you to go at once! He thinks she will die if you cannot get there. Here is a note."

"Wait," he said, "I will come."

He shut the window, and was soon at the door.

"The worst of it is," the doctor said, "that my horse has been out all day and is quite tired. May I have your horse?"

"He has come at a gallop nearly all the way, sir, and I was to give him a rest here," said John. "But I think Mr. Gordon would agree to it. Beauty will take you back."

"All right," Doctor White said. "I will soon be right down."

John stood by me and stroked my neck. I was already very hot. The doctor came out with his riding whip.

"You need not take that, sir," said John. "Black Beauty will run for you. Take care of him, sir. I would not like any harm to come to him."

In a minute we had left John far behind.

The doctor was a heavier man than John, and not so good a rider. However, I did my very best and ran as fast I could.

When we got home, Joe led me to the stable. My legs were shaking under me and I could only stand and pant. I had not a dry hair on my body. Water ran down my legs, and I steamed all over.

Joe came to attend to me and he rubbed my legs and chest. Poor Joe! I'm sure he did what he thought was best, but he knew very little about taking care of a hot and tired horse. He did not put my warm blanket on me because he thought that I was too hot and would not like it. Then he gave me a pail of water. It was cold and very good and I drank it all. He gave me some hay and some corn. Thinking he had done right, he went away.

Soon I began to shake and tremble. I turned deadly cold. My legs ached and so did my loins and chest. I felt sore all over. I wished for my warm blanket as my shaking legs gave out. I wished for John, but he was walking home from the doctor's. I lay down in my straw and tried to sleep.

After a long while I heard John at the door. I gave a low moan, for I was in great pain. He was at my side in a moment. I couldn't tell him how I felt, but he seemed to know. He covered me and ran for some hot water. He mashed some oats in warm water. I ate it, and then I went to sleep.

I was now very ill. My chest hurt and I could not breathe without pain. John nursed me night and day, getting up two or three times in the night to come to me. Squire Gordon also came to see me often.

"My poor Beauty," the Squire said one day. "My good horse, you saved Mistress Gordon's life. Yes, you saved her life."

John told him that he had never seen a horse go so fast. "It was almost as if he knew why we were going," he said. Of course I *did* know. I knew that we had to run for Mistress Gordon's sake.

I do not know how long I was ill. The horse doctor came every day. One night John had to give me some medicine. Young Joe's father came in to help him. After I had taken the medicine they stayed with me.

Joe's father spoke in a low voice. "Joe is broken-hearted. He is unable to eat his meals and he never smiles now. He says it is his fault if Beauty dies. I wish you would say a word to him to make him feel better."

John said slowly, "I'll try to give him a good word tomorrow if Beauty is better. I know he meant no harm. I know he is a good boy. I cannot bear to see Beauty lose her life because he did the wrong thing. Not knowing the *right* thing to do often does more harm in this world than wickedness itself."

I heard no more, for the medicine made me sleep. In the morning I felt much better. I added John's speech to the words I remembered when I came to know more of the world.

CHAPTER SEVEN

The Parting

I had now lived in this happy place for three years. Sad changes were about to come over us.

We had heard from time to time that Mistress Gordon was ill, and the doctor was often at the house. Squire Gordon looked grave and worried. Now the doctor said she must leave England. She would go to a warm country for two or three years. The doctor thought this would make her well.

The news fell upon the household like a storm. Everyone in the house and in the stable was heartbroken. John went about his work silent and sad. Joe no longer whistled. Nothing else was talked about in the stable.

There was a great deal of coming and going.
Ginger and I were kept busy.

The Squire began to make plans to leave
their home. He gave Merrylegs to their minister,
Mr. Bloomfield. The minister's children knew
and loved Merrylegs. The little pony was never
to be sold. He would just stay in their field when
he became too old to work. Joe Green was hired
to take care of Merrylegs and help in the
Bloomfields' house. I was pleased to know that
Merrylegs was to be happy, but Ginger and I
were worried about what was to happen to us.

Miss Jessie and Miss Flora came to tell us
good-bye. They hugged Merrylegs and called
him a good friend. They were no longer afraid to
touch Ginger, and they patted Ginger and me.
But now they would not bring treats or pat us
ever again. Once more we all felt very sad.

Now we heard that the Squire had sold
Ginger and me to his friend, the Earl of Wilburn.

"You will have a good home there," he told us.

The evening before he left, Squire Gordon
came into the stable. He wanted to pet us for the
last time. I could tell from the tone of his voice
that he was in very low spirits.

"Have you decided what to do, John?" he asked. "You have had many offers to work. I see that you have not taken any of them."

"No, sir, I have not," John answered. "I have made up my mind to find a job with a good horse trainer. Too many young colts are frightened by wrong treatment. That need not be if they are treated gently. I shall feel as if I am doing some good. What do you think of it, sir?"

"You will be good at that job," answered the Squire. "You understand horses, and somehow they understand you. I think you could not do better. If in any way I can help you, please write to me."

The Squire gave John the address, and then he thanked him for his long and faithful service.

John said, "We will never forget you, sir. We hope that someday Mistress Gordon will be well. We hope that you can come back to England again."

Squire Gordon shook hands with John. I thought that John had spoken words for Ginger and me. I was grateful to him since I could not speak.

The last sad day came. Ginger and I pulled the carriage up to the house for the last time. The servants brought out cushions and blankets and many other things. Then Squire Gordon came down the steps carrying Mistress Gordon in his arms and placed her carefully in the carriage. The servants cried as they said good-bye.

"Good-bye," he said to them. "We shall not forget any of you." Then he got in the carriage. "Drive on, John," he called.

We trotted slowly to the gate and down through the village. People stood at their doors to watch our last journey. They called out, "Blessings on you."

At the railway station, Squire Gordon held Mistress Gordon while she patted us. "Good-bye, Ginger and Beauty," she said. "Good-bye, John. Blessings on you."

I felt the reins twitch, but John did not say anything. I think that he was too sad to speak. Joe took the things out of the carriage. Then John asked him to stand by us while he went to wait for the train.

Poor Joe! He stood very close to our heads to hide his tears.

Very soon the train came puffing up to the station. In two or three minutes the doors were slammed shut and it glided away. Only clouds of white smoke—and some very heavy hearts—were left behind it.

When it was out of sight, John came back. "We shall never see her again," he said. "Never."

He took the reins from Joe and drove slowly home. But it was not our home now.

CHAPTER EIGHT

Earlshall

The next morning after breakfast, Joe told us good-bye and he and Merrylegs went to the Bloomfields', with Merrylegs neighing a farewell to us. Then John put the saddle on Ginger and the leading rein on me, and walked us across the country to Earlshall Park, where the Earl lived.

We were taken to a light, airy stable, and placed in stalls next to each other, where we were rubbed down and fed. Shortly, John and Mister York, our new groom, came in to see us.

"Mister Manly, is there anything about either of these horses that I need to know?"

"Well," said John, "I don't believe there is a

better pair of horses in the country. They work well together, but they are not alike. The black one has the most perfect temper I ever knew. Ginger is a more jumpy horse than the black. Flies irritate her more. Anything wrong in her harness upsets her. If she is not treated right she may kick or bite. There is another thing you should know. These horses have never worn a checkrein. It holds their heads up too high and is not comfortable for them."

"Well," York said, "they must wear it here. It is the fashion and Lady Wilburn insists that they wear it. Their heads must be pulled up tightly. She *will* have fashion."

John looked sad when he came to say goodbye. I held my face close to him. That was all I could do. Then he was gone and I have never seen him since.

The next day the Earl came to look us over. In the afternoon we were fastened to the carriage. York put a stiff leather checkrein on us but he did not fasten it too tightly on our necks. It did not pull my head up higher than I usually held it. We went to the front of the Earl's fine big house.

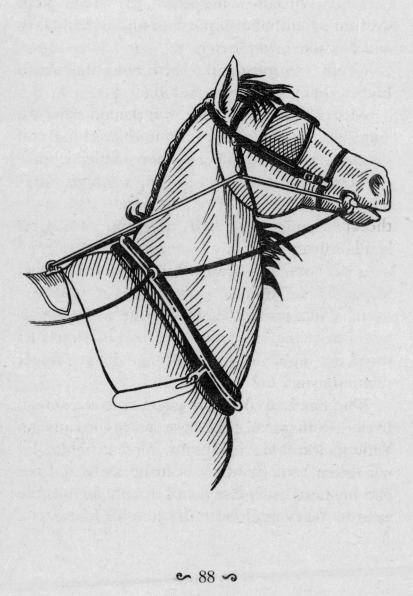

Lady Wilburn came down the stone steps dressed in silk. She stepped around to look at us and did not seem pleased.

"York, you must make them hold their heads higher. They must be in fashion."

Mister York said, "I beg your pardon, my lady. They are just getting used to the checkrein. But if you wish, I will pull their heads up a little higher."

"Do so," she said.

Mister York came to our heads and made the checkreins tighter. It made our necks and heads uncomfortable.

The next day, Lady Wilburn insisted that Mister York shorten the checkreins to force our heads even higher. Every day our checkreins were shortened to please the lady. I began to dread getting my head pulled up so high. Ginger seemed upset, but she was quiet.

One day Lady Wilburn came down later than usual. "You must get those horses' heads up higher," she said. "Do it now."

Mister York drew my head up and fixed the checkrein so tightly that my neck hurt. He went to Ginger. When he tried to shorten the checkrein,

she reared up, knocking his hat off. York went to her head, but she was out of control. She rose up and plunged down over and over, and then she reared and kicked.

At last she kicked herself away from the carriage and fell down.

Mister York sat on her head to keep her from hurting herself. He yelled for someone to get us loose from the carriage. A groom led me to my stall. He just turned me in as I was and ran back to Ginger. My head was still pulled up and I could not get it down—even to eat. I was miserable. I had never kicked in life, but at that moment, I was ready to kick the first person who came near me.

Before long, Ginger was led in. She looked bruised and still upset. Mister York came and let down my head. It felt so good to be able to move it as I wished.

Ginger was never harnessed to the carriage again. The Earl's son took her to ride when he hunted foxes or deer. I worked with another horse until the Earl's family went to London. They left us in the care of Reuben Smith, who was one of the grooms.

Two of the family remained at home. The Lady Harriet was often ill, but the Lady Anne loved to ride horseback. She was as cheerful and gentle as she was beautiful. She chose me for her horse and named me "Black Auster."

One day Lady Anne and her cousin Collin Blantyre, who was visiting, rode out. Lady Anne decided to ride Collin's horse, a mare named Lizzie. Lizzie was beautiful and had a fine spirit, but she was easily upset. Collin rode me.

Just as we were moving off, a servant came out with a slip of paper. Lady Harriet wanted us to ask a question for her at Dr. Ashley's.

The village was about a mile off, and Dr. Ashley's house was on the far side of it. We went along well, enjoying the day. At Dr. Ashley's gate, Collin hung my rein on one of the iron spikes. He told Lady Anne he would be out soon, and then he took the paper inside.

Lizzie was standing quietly by the side of the road a few feet away from me. The Lady Anne was on her, holding her reins loosely.

There was a meadow on the opposite side of the road. Suddenly, a boy drove out some young colts. He was cracking a whip and making them run wildly. One of them ran across the road and bumped Lizzie's legs.

Lizzie was startled and she kicked and dashed off in a wild gallop. It was so sudden that Lady Anne nearly fell from the horse. She stayed

in the saddle, but could not bring Lizzie to a stop.

I gave a shrill neigh for help. Again and again I neighed. I pawed the ground and tossed my head to get the rein loose. Collin came running to the gate. He saw the flying figure, now far away on the road. He sprang into the saddle, and we dashed after them.

For about a mile and a half the road ran straight. Then it divided into two roads. Long before we came to the two roads, Lizzie was out of sight. A woman was standing at her garden gate.

"Which way?" Collin shouted.

"To the right," the woman cried.

Away we went, up the right-hand road. For a moment we saw her. Then she raced around another bend. A man was standing near a heap of stones patching the road. He dropped his shovel and waved to us.

"Go to the common fields. She has turned off there," he shouted.

This field, which was used by everyone, had very uneven ground. It was covered with heather and bushes. There was an open space with anthills and mole holes everywhere. It was the worst place I knew for a horse to run.

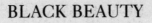

We could see them when we came to the field. Lady Anne's hat was gone. Her long brown hair flew out behind her. Her head and body were thrown back. She was pulling with all her strength to stop Lizzie.

A wide ditch had been cut in the field, with the earth from the ditch thrown up to form a bank on the other side. I hoped that the ditch would halt Lizzie and let me catch them, but it did not. Lizzie took the jump across the ditch without slowing down. She landed among the rough clods, and fell.

Collin groaned. "Now, Auster, do your best!"

I gathered myself together. With one great jump, I cleared both ditch and bank.

Lady Anne lay very still among the heather with her face turned to the ground. Collin kneeled down and turned her face upward. She was very pale and her eyes were closed.

Two men were cutting grass near us. Seeing Lizzie running wild without a rider, they left their work to catch her. Then the men came to help us. Collin told one of the men to ride me to Doctor Ashley's. We ran on to Earlshall to tell them to send a carriage and Lady Anne's maid.

There was a great deal of hurry and excitement at the Hall. I was put into my stall, the saddle and bridle taken off, and a blanket thrown over me. Ginger was saddled and sent off. She was gone a long time.

"We got there just as the doctor did," Ginger told me after she was returned to the stable and we were left alone. "Lady Anne was lying with her head in a woman's lap. Her eyes were closed, but I heard someone say that she wasn't dead. After a while she was put into the carriage and we came home."

Two days after the accident, Collin paid me a visit. He patted me and praised me.

"I am sure he knew of Lady Anne's danger," he told Reuben Smith. "I couldn't have held him in, if I had tried. She ought not to ride any other horse."

He said that Lady Anne was now nearly healed. She would soon be able to ride again.

CHAPTER NINE

Broken Knees

Reuben Smith was a good groom and a first-rate driver. He was gentle and took very good care of the horses. Everyone liked him, but he had one great fault. That was the love of drink. He would not drink for months. Then he would take one drink. He would then take another and another until he was drunk.

One day, Reuben Smith was sent to town to carry out an errand for Lady Harriet. After he had done his errand, he rode me to a tavern. He ordered the groom there to have me ready at four o'clock. Smith came at five and said he had met some friends and that we wouldn't be leaving until six.

A nail in one of my front shoes had come loose. The groom asked Smith if he should have the shoe nailed back on.

"No," Smith answered. "It will be all right until we get home."

He went back into the tavern. I thought it was very unlike him to leave a nail loose.

It was nearly nine o'clock before he called for me. He spoke in a loud, rough voice that I had not heard before. He seemed in a bad temper.

As soon as we were out of town, he put me to a gallop. He gave me a sharp cut with his whip, though I was already racing through the night. The moon had not yet risen and it was very dark. The road was full of sharp stones, which loosened my shoe all the more, making it hard to run on that foot. At last I felt the shoe fly off.

If Smith had been sober he would have stopped and looked at my foot. He was too madly drunk to care for me.

I had to gallop over sharp stones with one shoe off. Smith cut me with his whip, and yelled at me to go faster. The hoof of my shoeless foot broke and split. My foot was terribly cut by the sharpness of the stones.

No horse could have stayed on his feet. The pain of my foot was too great. I stumbled and fell hard on both my knees. Smith was flung off. At the speed I was going, he must have fallen with great force. I soon stood up and limped to the side of the road. The moon had just risen and by its light I could see Smith. He lay without moving a few yards from me.

I was suffering intense pain in my foot and both front knees. This road was not much used. At this time of night we might wait hours for help. I stood watching and listening.

It was a calm, sweet April night. There were no sounds except for the low song of a nightingale. Nothing moved but the white clouds near the moon, and a brown owl that flew by. It made me think of summer nights long ago in Farmer Grey's meadow. I wished I could lie once again beside my mother in our pleasant meadow near the pond.

It must have been midnight when I thought I heard Ginger's step. I neighed loudly, and was glad to hear a neigh from Ginger. She pulled a cart with Robert and Ned from the stables riding in it. They got down and raised Reuben Smith

up, but he didn't move.

"He is dead," Robert said. "Feel how cold his hands are."

They laid him down again and came to look at me.

"Why, the horse has been down and thrown him!" Ned called. "Why would the black horse have done that?"

"It is strange that this horse hasn't moved," Robert said.

He then tried to lead me forward. I made a step but almost fell again.

"Look here," he said, "he has hurt his foot as well as his knees. His hoof is all cut to pieces. No wonder he fell. Smith would only ride him like this if he were drinking again. It is good that we were sent to look for them when they failed to return home."

They put the body in the cart. Robert came to look at my foot again. He bound his handkerchief closely about my foot. Then he led me home very slowly. I shall never forget that night walk. It was more than three miles. I limped on as well as I could with great pain. Robert often patted and encouraged me on the way.

At last I reached my own stall. Robert wrapped my knees in wet cloths. He tied up my foot with wet bran to cleanse it and draw out the heat. I managed to get myself down on the straw. I slept in spite of the pain.

The next day the horse doctor treated my wounds. He said that if my knee joints healed I could work again—but that my knees would always be ugly. There was nothing he could do about the scars.

It took a long time for my knees and

foot to heal and I was often in pain. When I could walk again I was put into a small meadow to rest. I enjoyed the liberty and the sweet grass, but I felt lonely. Then one morning the gate opened and Ginger came in.

I trotted up to her with a happy whinny. We put our heads close together to greet each other. She told me sadly that she had been brought in to rest from hard riding.

The Earl's son had ridden her in a race when her muscles were sore.

With her high spirits, she kept up with the fastest horses. But her rider was too heavy for her, and both her lungs and her back were hurt.

"And so," she said, "here we are, ruined in the prime of our youth. You by a drunkard, and I by a fool."

We didn't gallop about as we once did. We fed, and lay down together. We stood for hours under one of the shady trees with our heads close together. We heard the Earl and Mister York say that Ginger would need to rest for a year to heal. Then they said that I must be sold, for my knees were too ugly now for me to pull the Earl's carriage. It was not proper fashion to keep a horse whose knees had scars.

"They will take you away," said Ginger, "and I shall lose the only friend I have. Most likely we will never see each other again. It is a hard world."

One day Robert came into the field with a halter. He slipped it over my head.

There was no good-bye to Ginger. We neighed to each other as I was led off. She trotted along by the fence, calling to me. I answered her calls until I was too far away to hear them.

CHAPTER TEN

A London Cab Horse

I was bought by a man who kept several horses, which he rented out to different drivers. I was driven by many kinds of drivers. Some were kind and thoughtful and drove well. Some knew nothing about horses and cared nothing for my needs. I was driven over rough roads with a stone in my foot. I was flogged while I tried to pull heavy loads up high hills.

Later I was sold to a man who wanted a horse to ride. He meant well, but he was very busy. He left me in the care of foolish grooms. When they failed to feed and clean me, he was angry. He decided it was too much trouble to keep a horse, and I was sent to a horse fair to be sold again.

The horse fair was a very social event, as well as a place of business. There were horses and ponies of all kinds. Buyers were looking them all over and making offers. I was lucky. The man who bought me was the one I would have picked—had I been able to choose my owner.

I heard someone call him Jerry. He was a small man who showed that he knew all about horses. He rubbed my nose in a friendly way.

"Well, my friend, I think we'll get along," he said.

He saddled me and rode me into London. When we arrived, the gas lamps were already shining from the lamp stands on the streets. We rode through miles of crisscrossing streets. I thought we would never find our way. At last we turned onto a side street and stopped. I soon knew that this was my new owner's home. He whistled and his wife and a boy and a girl came out.

"Open the gate, Harry," he called to his son. "And bring the lantern please, Polly," he called to his wife.

He rode me into a small stable yard and got down. Soon they were all standing around me.

"Is he gentle?" asked the little girl.

My owner smiled and hugged her. "Just as gentle as he can be, Dolly. Pat him as much as you wish."

Her small hands felt good on my face and I stood very still for her.

My new family was happy and loving to each

other. Harry was nearly twelve years old and Dolly was eight. Jerry drove his own cab and owned another horse called Captain. He drove Captain in the mornings. In the afternoons Captain rested while I pulled the cab. On Sundays we both rested. Jerry refused to work on Sunday in order to spend the day with his family.

Jerry cared for us himself with Harry's help. He drove so well that I lost my fear of the noisy, crowded London streets. He cared nothing for fashion and never used a checkrein to force my head too high.

He talked with his family about my name. "He is a good horse," Jerry said. "He reminds me of our Jack before he became too old to pull a cab. Shall we call him Jack?"

"Let's do," said Polly. "It will seem like old times."

So Jack became my name.

I never knew a better man than my new owner. He was kind and good, and always did the right thing for everyone. He was very fond of making little songs, and singing them to himself.

> *"Come, father and mother,*
> *And sister and brother,*
> *Come, all of you, turn to*
> *And help one another."*

And so they did. Harry fed us and kept our stable clean. Polly and Dolly helped with the cab. They brushed and beat the dust from the cushions, and washed the glass. Jerry cleaned us in the yard while they worked.

There was a great deal of laughing and fun between them. It made Captain and me happy that we heard no scolding nor hard words.

They were always up early in the morning, for Jerry would sing,

> *"If you in the morning throw minutes away,*
> *You can't pick them up in the course of a day.*
> *You may hurry and scurry, and flurry and worry,*
> *You've lost them forever, forever and aye."*

He couldn't bear the waste of time. He refused to run us at top speed to get some careless person to a train on time. But he would do anything to help someone who was in real need.

Near noon one day, a young man who was carrying a piece of heavy luggage fell in the street. Jerry helped him up.
The young man walked as if
he were in great pain.

"I must get on the twelve o'clock train," he said. "This fall has made me late. I must make this trip. I will pay you extra."

"I would never race Jack for extra money," Jerry said. "He and I will get you there for your need. Now then, Jack, we will show how we can get through the streets."

At noontime in London the streets are full of carriages, carts, and cabs. Big wagons meet each other on the narrow streets. Their wheels come so close that another inch and they would scrape. Jerry and I were used to traffic. No one could go as well in it as we. I was bold and quick. Jerry could see an opening in the traffic and guide me into it.

We were blocked on London Bridge for several minutes. The young man put his head out.

"I might be better to get out and walk," he said. "I'm afraid we won't get there in time if this goes on."

Jerry told him that we would be on time. The cart in front of me began to move. We went in and out through the traffic at a quick trot. I found myself enjoying it. We whirled into the station just in time.

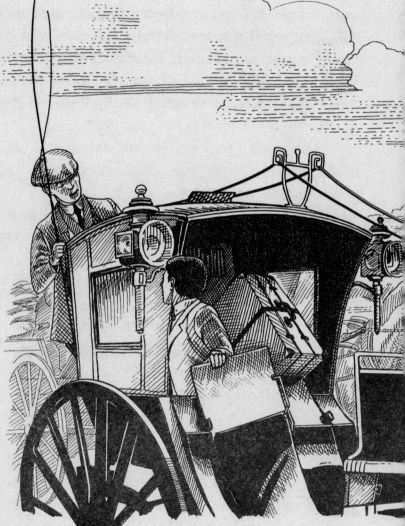

Jerry's fellow drivers at the cabstand teased him.

"You said you would never drive Jack hard for extra money," they said. "And here you did."

He let them joke for a while. Then he told them that we did it for the thanks of the young man.

"And," he added, "Jack and I thought that running fast that time was worth the effort. That man was late by no fault of his own."

As for me, I was fed extra rations. I thought of the fast dash through traffic as good experience. I knew that Jerry wouldn't ask it of me often.

CHAPTER ELEVEN

The Golden Rule

Jerry had a rule that his horses and his family should rest on Sunday. But there came a day when he broke his rule. Polly came into the yard one Sunday where he was grooming Captain and me.

"Young Dinah Brown's brother has sent her a message. Her mother is dying. She must go now to tell her good-bye. It is more than ten miles into the country. She asked me if you might take her. I do know we all are sorry to miss our Sunday."

Jerry stood silently for a moment. "We are and the horses need their rest. Still, I wouldn't want to know that I kept her from a last good-bye. We do as we want to be done by. Tell her that Jack and I will pick her up very soon."

Jerry borrowed a light cart, which made the trip much easier. We were soon out of the city and the soft country roads felt good to my feet. It was a fine May day. The air was sweet, and the green grass looked good. I began to feel quite fresh.

Dinah's family lived in a small farmhouse. We went up a green lane, close by a meadow, with some fine shady trees. Dinah's brother offered to take me to a cowshed.

"I wish I had a better stable to offer," he said.

"I know that my horse would like to have an hour or two in your pretty meadow. It would be a real treat for him," Jerry said.

"Take him there and welcome." Then he invited Jerry in to eat a meal with the family.

"I have sandwiches with me," Jerry said. "I would enjoy walking in the meadow as much as my horse."

When Jerry took my harness off I didn't know what I should do first. Should I roll over on my back or lie down and rest? Should I eat the grass?

Should I gallop across the meadow out of glad spirits at being free? In the end, I did them all by turns. I enjoyed each of them very much.

Jerry seemed quite as happy as I was. He sat down under a shady tree and listened to the birds sing. He sang some songs himself. He read out of a brown book I knew he liked very much. He wandered around the meadow and down by a little brook. He picked wildflowers and tied them up with long sprays of ivy.

But the time seemed all too short. I had not run free since I left Ginger back at Earlshall.

When we got back to London, Jerry gave Polly the flowers. "I didn't miss my Sunday after all," he told her. "The birds were singing hymns in every bush. As for Jack, he was like a young colt again."

That time in the country left me thinking about Ginger. I wondered where she might be. But when I learned the truth about her one day, I was sorry to know it.

The winter came in early, cold and wet. There was snow, or sleet, or rain almost every day. The horses and drivers all felt the freezing winds and frosts very much.

One day while I waited for Jerry, a worn out cab came up beside me. The horse was a scrawny old chestnut. Her bones showed through her ill-kept coat. Her legs were shaky and her eyes dull. I was eating some hay and when the wind blew a few straws her way, she stretched out her thin neck and ate it. Then she looked around for more.

I thought that I had seen that poor creature before. I tried to remember where.

"Black Beauty, my old friend," she called. "Is it really you? Do you not remember me?"

It was Ginger! What had happened to her? Her neck was drooping. I could see the painful swelling in her joints. Her face that was once full of spirit was now full of suffering. Her thin sides shook as she drew in her breath. She coughed often.

"Ginger," I cried. "What has been done to you?"

"My life has not been good," she said. "After resting at Earlshall, I was forced to run again. I lost all my strength and was too weak to race or hunt. I was sold from owner to owner. And now I am here, just being used up by cab drivers. They pay my owner for my use every day. They push me hard with no rest and little food. I wish the end was come. I wish I was dead."

"You used to stand up for yourself if you were abused."

"It is of no use," she said. "Men are strongest. There is nothing we horses can do."

I rubbed my nose to hers. It was all I could do to tell her how sorry I was.

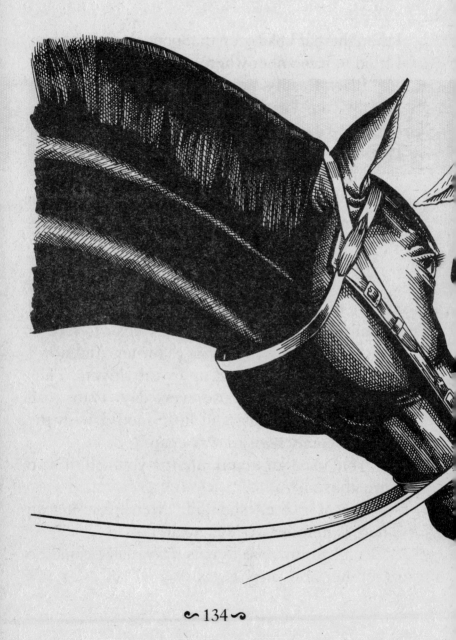

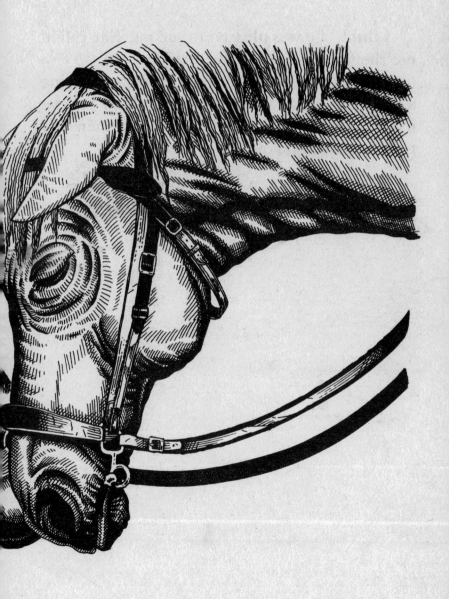

I think she was pleased to see me. She called me the only friend she ever had.

A short time after this, I passed a cart carrying a dead horse that was of Ginger's color. I believe it was Ginger. I hoped it was, for then her troubles would be over.

Jerry's New Year

Election Day kept Jerry and me busy carrying people from place to place. The streets were very full. The cabs were dashing about through the crowds. As soon as we left one customer, another got in our cab.

When we stopped for a moment, Jerry gave me my oats. "We must eat when we can," he said. "Munch away, Jack, and enjoy your lunch, old boy."

Jerry took out one of Polly's meat pies to eat. Just then a young woman came along the street carrying a sick child. She was looking about and seemed to be lost.

"Please can you tell me the way to St. Thomas's

hospital?" she begged. "I need to get my poor boy to the hospital. Poor little fellow, he suffers a great deal of pain."

"The hospital is three miles away," Jerry said. "Get in the cab, and Jack and I will take you there."

"I can't do that, sir, though I thank you," she said. "I have no money to pay you."

"You might be knocked down in these crowded streets," said Jerry. "The child might be run over. I have a wife and dear children at home. I know a father's feelings. Get in the cab. There will be no charge for you."

We were soon on our way. The woman blessed Jerry over and over before she took her son inside the hospital.

Just as we were leaving, a lady came out of the hospital and called out to us. She smiled when she saw Jerry.

"Jeremiah!" she called out. "I'm very glad to find a friend like you. I would have had trouble getting a cab on Election Day."

"I'm pleased that I happened to be here, Mistress Fowler," Jerry said. "Where may I carry you?"

"To the train station. And tell me all the news of your wife and children."

They talked, and I learned that Polly had once worked for Mistress Fowler. "I know the work of a cab driver is hard," she said as she left us. "If you should ever want to give it up, let me know."

In Christmas week, Jerry had a bad cough, but he drove his cab all week. On New Year's eve, at nine o'clock, we took two gentlemen to a house. We were told to come back at eleven o'clock.

"It is a card party," said one of them. "You may have to wait a few minutes, but don't be late."

We were at the door at eleven, for Jerry was never late. But the two men were not so thoughtful. It was twelve o'clock, and they still had not come.

The wind had been blowing squalls of rain all day. Now a sharp driving sleet came on. It was very cold and there was no shelter.

Jerry pulled my blanket closer over me. "I'm sorry, old friend," he said. "When we have taken them home, I will take you to your stall."

He walked up and down, stamping his feet. That set him off coughing. Still no one came. He rang the bell to ask if he would be wanted that night.

"Oh, yes, you will be wanted," he was told. "You must not go. The game will soon be over."

Again Jerry came back to the cab. He was now so hoarse that I could hardly hear him.

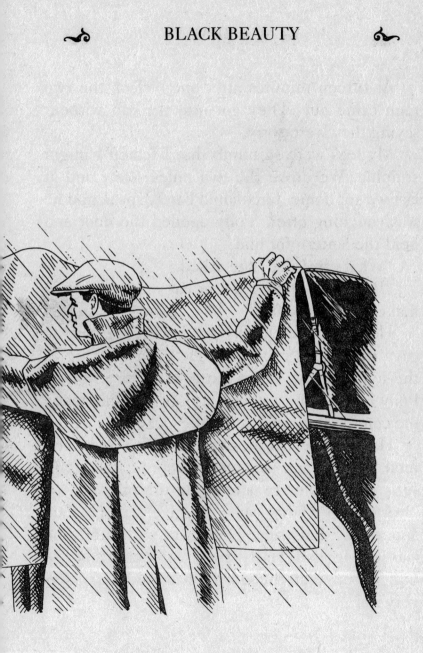

At fifteen minutes after one o'clock the two men came out. They got into the cab without saying they were sorry.

My legs were so numb that I feared I might stumble. We drove the two miles safely and at last we got home. Jerry could barely speak and he was coughing often. Polly opened the door and held the lantern for him.

"What can I do?" she asked.

"Please get Jack a warm oat mash and then make me some soup."

He could now hardly get his breath, but he gave me a good rub-down. He even went up to the loft to throw down extra straw for my bed. Polly brought me a warm mash of oats that made me comfortable, and then they locked the door.

Harry came the next morning to clean and feed Captain and me, and sweep out the stalls. Jerry didn't come to take us out to work.

At noon Harry came to give us our feed and water. This time Dolly was with him. She was crying and Harry tried to comfort her. I understood that the doctor had said Jerry was very sick.

Three days passed and I only saw Harry. On the third day one of the other cab drivers came to the stable.

"I want to ask how your father is," he told Harry.

"He is very bad," said Harry. "The doctor thinks we will know tonight if he will live."

The man patted Harry's shoulder. "While there is life, there is hope. Keep up your spirits."

"Yes, we try," said Harry. "I believe the doctor thinks that Father will get well."

The man nodded. "If there is any rule that good men should get well, I am sure he will. Jerry is the best man I know. I will look in again tomorrow."

Early the next morning he was there.

"How is he?" he asked.

"He is better," said Harry happily. "Mother hopes he will get well."

Jerry did get better, but the doctor said he must never go back to cab work again.

One day Dolly came dancing into the stable. "Oh, Harry, remember Mistress Fowler? Father drove her from the hospital on Election Day. She has written to us. She says that we are all to go and live near her. There's a cottage with a garden and apple trees. Father will drive her carriage."

This was sad news for me. I was no longer young. Cab work, even with the best driver, will tear down one's strength. I felt that I wasn't the horse I had been. I knew that I couldn't expect another owner as good as Jerry.

Because he was still so weak, Jerry wasn't allowed to go out before they moved to the country. I never saw him again after that New Year's eve. Polly and the children came to tell me good-bye.

"Dear old Jack," Polly said, putting her face close to my neck and kissing me. "I wish we could take you with us."

Dolly was crying and she kissed me, too. Harry stroked me a great deal, but said nothing, only he seemed very sad. And so I was led away to my new place.

CHAPTER THIRTEEN

Hard Times

I was sold to a baker whom Jerry knew. He thought I would have a good home with him. If my new owner had always been around, I believe I would have been treated better. But he was away much of the time. The baker had a foreman who was always rushing to get their orders delivered. He often had more weight put on when I already had a full load.

He was not concerned with my comfort, and I had my head forced up too high with a checkrein. This kept me from pulling well. I felt my strength beginning to fail from the overwork.

One day, I was loaded down more than usual.

We came to a steep hill and I had to use all my strength to try to pull the load. The strain was so much that I had to stop several times. Then my driver, whose name was Jakes, whipped me.

"Get on, you lazy fellow," Jakes said. "I will flog you until you do."

I wasn't able to move the load as fast as Jakes wanted. He whipped me cruelly. My mind was hurt as much as my poor sides. It was hard to be abused when I was doing my best, and it took the spirit out of me when he whipped me again.

A lady was walking on a path beside the road. She stopped and said in a sweet voice, "Oh, please don't whip your horse again. Your load is so heavy and the road is very steep."

"My foreman put the load on and I must get it delivered." Jakes raised his whip again.

"Please," the lady said, "you are not giving him a fair chance. He cannot use all his strength with his head pulled up so high. I would be so glad if you would take the checkrein off."

"Well," said Jakes, with a short laugh, "anything to please a lady."

He took the rein off. I put my head down near my knees. What a comfort it was.

"This is what he wanted," said the lady. She came off the path to the road. She stroked my neck and patted me. Her gentle hand felt good, as I had not been patted for many a long day.

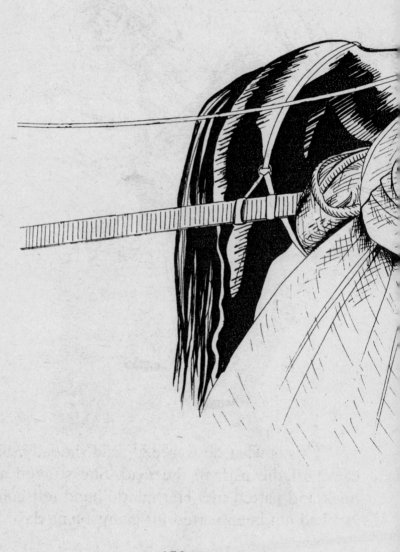

"Now speak kindly to him and lead him. I believe he will be able to do better."

Jakes took my rein, saying, "Come on, Blackie."

I put down my head. I threw my whole weight against the load and spared no strength. The load moved and I pulled it steadily up the hill. The lady walked beside us.

"You see," she said, "he was quite willing. You just had to give him the chance. You won't put that checkrein on again, will you?"

Jakes was getting ready to hitch the rein up again. "Well, ma'am, having his head free has helped him. I'll remember that when we have a hill to climb. I thank you, ma'am. But I must keep his head pulled up. It is the fashion. I would be laughed at if I left the checkrein off all the time."

"Is it not better," she said, "to *lead* a good fashion than to *follow* a bad one? We have no right to hurt any animals. We call them dumb animals and they are only dumb in the sense that they

cannot talk. They hurt no *less*, simply because they cannot *speak* to us. I thank you for trying my plan with your horse. I won't keep you any longer. Good-day."

With a last soft pat on my neck she stepped away. I never saw her again.

After that, Jakes did keep my checkrein looser and he took it off when we went uphill. But still the foreman put too many heavy loads on me. Good food and enough rest will keep up one's strength under fair work, but no horse can stand against overloading. I became worn out from the loads. A younger horse was bought in my place. I was sold to a large cab owner.

I shall never forget this new owner. He had black eyes and a hooked nose, his mouth was as full of teeth as a bulldog's, and his voice was as harsh as cart wheels scraping over rocks. His name was Nicholas Skinner.

I have heard men say that seeing is believing. I should say that *feeling* is believing. I had seen much before. I never knew until now the misery of a cab horse's life.

Skinner had a ragged set of cabs and a ragged set of drivers. He was hard on the men, and the

men, in turn, were hard on the horses. It was in the heat of summer, and we were given little rest. We never had a Sunday off. The work was hard and the loads could be heavy. We often had to take a large group into the country.

My driver had a cruel whip. It had something so sharp on the end that it sometimes drew blood. He would flip the lash out at my head, which caused such pain that it took the heart out of me. Still, I did my best and never hung back. As poor Ginger said, it was no use. Men are strongest.

I was in misery. I wished I might drop down dead at my work. I wished only to be free of my misery, as Ginger was. One day my wish very nearly came to pass.

I went on the cabstand at eight in the morning and I had already done a good share of work by midday. Then we went to pick up people who were coming on the train. After the heavy train pulled into the station, a noisy man with a lady and a young boy and girl came up to our cab. They had a great deal of luggage. The lady and the boy got into the cab. The little girl came and looked at me.

"Papa," she said, "this poor horse is weak and worn out. I'm sure he cannot take us and all our bags so far."

"Oh, he's all right, Miss," said my driver. "He's strong enough."

A large number of heavy boxes were being loaded and someone suggested taking a second cab. My driver insisted again that I could pull as much as they could pile on. He helped to load on a very heavy box. I could feel the springs of the cab go down.

"Papa, *do* take a second cab," the young girl begged. "I'm sure this is wrong and cruel."

"Nonsense, Grace, get in at once. Do not make all this fuss," the man ordered. "The driver knows whether or not his horse can pull us. Get in now and hold your tongue!"

My gentle friend had to do as she was told. Box after box was dragged up onto the cab. At last my driver yanked on the rein. He hit me with the whip and drove me out of the station.

I had been given neither food nor rest since early morning, but I did my best. I got along fairly well until we came to a great hill. There my weakness and the heavy load were too much.

I was trying hard to pull my load up the hill. All of a sudden, my feet slipped from under me and I fell. The force of my fall seemed to beat all the breath out of my body. I was unable to move and I thought that now I was going to die.

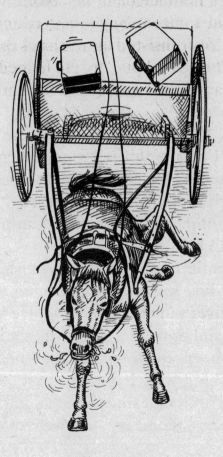

I heard a mix of angry voices and the sounds of boxes being unloaded. It was all like a dream. I thought I heard little Grace's voice saying, "Oh, that poor horse! It is all our fault."

Another voice said that I would never get up again. Someone came and loosened the straps of my harness. I didn't even open my eyes. I could only draw a gasping breath now and then.

CHAPTER FOURTEEN

Farmer Thoroughgood and Willie

I can't tell how long I lay there. At last I found my life coming back. A kind-voiced man asked me to rise, as he patted me gently. I tried hard, but at first I could not get my legs to raise me up. I tried again and this time I got to my feet. I was led to some nearby stables. Here I was put into a clean stall. Some warmed oats were brought to me. In the evening I was well enough to be led back to Skinner's stables, and in the morning a horse doctor came. He told Skinner that I would need a long rest.

"I have no meadows to nurse sick horses in," Skinner said. "I work my horses as long as they'll go. Then I sell them for whatever I can get."

So I was sent, once again, to the horse sales.

At the sale, I was placed with the old broken-down horses. The buyers and sellers looked not much better off than the sad beasts they were trading. There were poor old men hoping to buy a horse or pony for a few coins, to drag a wood or coal cart. Other poor men hoped to sell a worn-out beast for a little, rather than take the loss of killing him.

Some of them looked as if hard times had hardened them all over. There were others that I would have been glad to serve. They were poor and shabby, but kind and humane, with voices I could trust. There was one old man who took a fancy to me. I liked him, but I wasn't strong enough for his needs.

It was an anxious time for me. Who would take me now? Then a gentleman farmer with a young boy came from another part of the fair. They had been looking at the younger horses. The farmer had a broad back, round shoulders, and a kind face under a broad-brimmed hat. He and the young boy looked at us with pity. I saw his gaze rest on me. I pricked up my ears and looked at him.

"That horse has known better days, Willie," he said. He gave me a gentle pat on the neck. I put out my nose in answer to his kindness.

The boy stroked my face. "Poor old fellow! See, Grandpapa, how well he understands kindness. Could you buy him and make him young again? You made Ladybird young again."

"My dear boy, I can't make all old horses young. Besides, Ladybird wasn't so very old. She was run down and badly abused."

"Well, Grandpapa, I believe this one is not old, either. Look at his mane and tail. I wish you would look in his mouth. Then you could tell. His eyes aren't sunk like some old horses. He is just very thin."

The old gentleman laughed. "Bless the boy! He is as horsey as his old grandfather."

"The young boy is right," said the man who had brought me to the sale. "This horse is just worn down with cab work. The horse doctor said that a rest would make him well again."

The farmer slowly felt my legs, which were very swollen. Then he looked at my mouth. "Thirteen or fourteen years old, I should say. Just trot him out, will you?"

I arched my poor thin neck, raised my tail a little, and threw out my legs as well as I could, for they were very stiff. The farmer watched me. Then he paid the asking price. The boy was very happy, and the old gentleman seemed to enjoy his grandson's pleasure.

I was taken into the country and released into a large meadow. I learned that the old gentleman's name was Mr. Thoroughgood. He gave me over to the care of his groom and his grandson, Willie, who was fond of me. He and the groom took good care of me. The young boy was proud to be in charge of me and he came out every day to bring me a carrot or an apple. I became very fond of him, also. He called me Old Crony because I liked to come to him and follow him about.

The perfect rest, good food, the soft grass, and gentle exercise soon made me better. During the winter, my legs improved so much that I began to feel quite young again. One day in March, Willie and his grandfather hitched me to a small carriage and drove me a few miles. My legs were no longer stiff, and I did the work with perfect ease.

CHAPTER FIFTEEN

My Last Home

One day during the summer, the groom cleaned and brushed me carefully. I thought some new change must be at hand. Willie and his grandfather drove me to a pretty house. We followed a short driveway past a pretty lawn up to the door. Willie rang the bell. He asked if Miss Bloomfield or Miss Ellen was at home. Yes, they were.

Willie and I waited while Mr. Thoroughgood went into the house. He soon came back with three ladies. A tall, pale lady wore a white shawl. She leaned on a younger lady, who had a merry face. The third was a very stately-looking person.

Mr. Thoroughgood called her Miss Bloomfield. They all came and looked at me and asked questions.

"I am sure that I shall like him," said the younger one. "He has such a good face."

"But, Miss Ellen," said the tall lady, "he has fallen once. I would always be nervous riding behind him. I could never trust a horse that has fallen."

"You see, ladies," said Mr. Thoroughgood, "it is the careless drivers to blame. Many first-rate horses have had their knees broken. Many have had their health broken by poor or careless drivers. I think that is the case from what I see of this horse. If you wish, you may take the horse on trial. Your groom can see what he thinks of him."

The ladies agreed. "We will send for him tomorrow," said Miss Ellen.

In the morning, a smart-looking young man came for me. At first he looked pleased. When he saw my knees, he sounded unhappy. "I didn't think, sir, you would have sent a horse with bad knees to my ladies."

"Handsome is as handsome *does*," said Mr. Thoroughgood. "You are only taking him on trial.

I am sure you will be fair to him, young man. He is as safe as any horse you ever drove. If he is not, you may send him back."

I was led to the Bloomfields', placed in a comfortable stable, fed well—and then was left by myself. The next day my groom was cleaning my face when he stopped and stared at me for a moment.

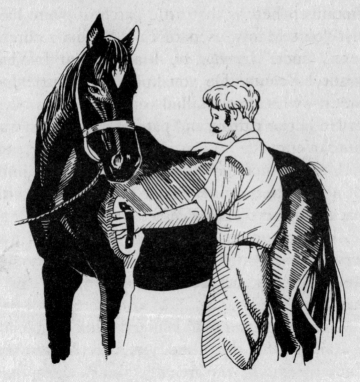

"That is just like the star that Black Beauty had. He was much the same height, too. I wonder where he is now."

He cleaned and brushed me more. He began to look me over carefully, talking to himself.

"White star in the forehead. One white foot on the right. This scar here. This little knot just in that place." Then he looked at my back. "As I'm alive, there is that little patch of white hair that John Manly used to call 'Beauty's three-penny spot.' It *must* be Black Beauty! Why, Beauty! Beauty! Do you know me? Little Joe Green—who almost killed you?"

He began patting and patting me as if he was quite overjoyed.

I could not say that I remembered him, for now he was a fine, grown young fellow, with black whiskers and a man's voice. But I was *sure* he knew *me*, and that he *was* Joe Green. I was very glad and put my nose up to him, to let him know that we were friends. I never saw a man so pleased.

"Give you a fair trial! I should think so indeed! I wonder who the rascal was that broke your knees, my old Beauty! You must have been badly treated somewhere. Well, well, you will have good times of it now. I wish that John Manly were here to see you."

In the afternoon, I was put to a low carriage and taken to the door. Miss Ellen was going to try me, and Joe Green went with her. I soon found that she was a good driver, and she seemed pleased with me. I heard Joe telling her about me, and that he was sure I was Squire Gordon's old Black Beauty.

When we returned, the other sisters came out to hear how I had done. Miss Ellen told them what Joe had said, and added with a smile, "I shall certainly write to Mrs. Gordon and tell her that her favorite horse has come to us. How pleased she will be!"

After this, I was driven every day for a week or so. Since I appeared to be quite safe, the lady who was frail and pale—Miss Lavinia—at last came out for a ride in a small carriage. It was quite decided after this happy day that the Bloomfields would keep me and call me by my old name of Black Beauty.

I have now lived in this happy place a whole year. Joe is the best and kindest of grooms. My work is easy and pleasant, and I feel my strength and spirits all coming back again. Mr. Thoroughgood said to Joe the other day:

"In your place he will live a long time. Until he is twenty years old—perhaps more."

Willie always speaks to me when he can and treats me as his special friend. My ladies have promised that I shall never be sold, and so I have nothing to fear.

Here my story ends. My troubles are all over, and I am at home.

Often before I am quite awake, I dream. I dream that I am back in the orchard at Birtwick Park, standing with my old friends under the apple trees.

THE END

ANNA SEWELL

Anna Sewell wrote only one book. While sick in bed, she penned the story that would become one of the most loved stories ever written, an autobiography of a gallant black horse— *Black Beauty*.

Anna was born in Great Yarmouth, Suffolk, England, in 1820. She grew up with a strong Quaker faith and a great love for horses. Sadly, a bone disease and a fall when she was only fourteen left her crippled. When she was older, she rode about in a pony cart—still enjoying the horses she adored.

In 1871, Anna was told she did not have many years left to live. Though very ill and confined to her bed, she wrote a story about a horse. Her wish was that this book would help people be kind to horses. Her story of Black Beauty, his many friends and owners, and his life of joys and hardships, was published in 1877. Anna died in 1878.

The Society for Prevention of Cruelty to Animals adopted and used *Black Beauty* to improve the treatment of animals everywhere.